Copyright 2016 Holley

Disclaimer- Although wrestling with your friends may seem like harmless fun, attempting to copy the moves done by professional wrestlers is extremely dangerous. Even with proper training, wrestlers can be seriously injured during their matches. **DO NOT TRY THIS AT HOME!**

This is a work of fiction. Names, characters, places and incidents either are products of the author's imagination or are used fictitiously. Any resemblance to actual events or locales or persons, living or dead, is entirely coincidental.

"One...Two...Three!!! *Mr. Madness* retains the Heavyweight Title. What a match!" Talking Tony announced.

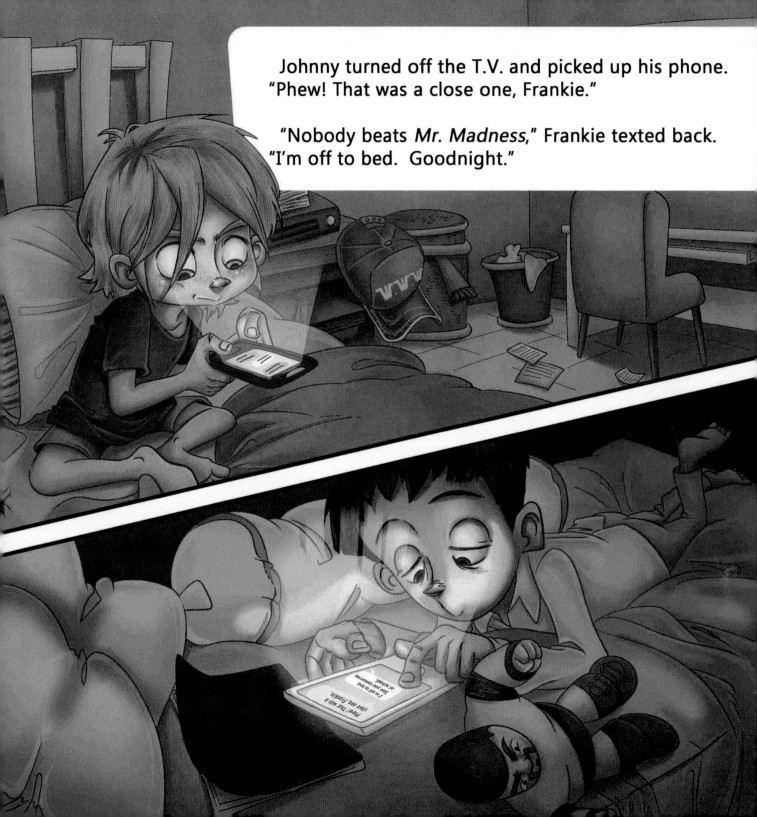

Johnny turned off the T.V. and picked up his phone. "Phew! That was a close one, Frankie."

"Nobody beats *Mr. Madness*," Frankie texted back. "I'm off to bed. Goodnight."

For as long as they could remember, the boys watched Wild, Wild Warriors, their favorite wrestling federation together.

Their weekly ritual started back in kindergarten.

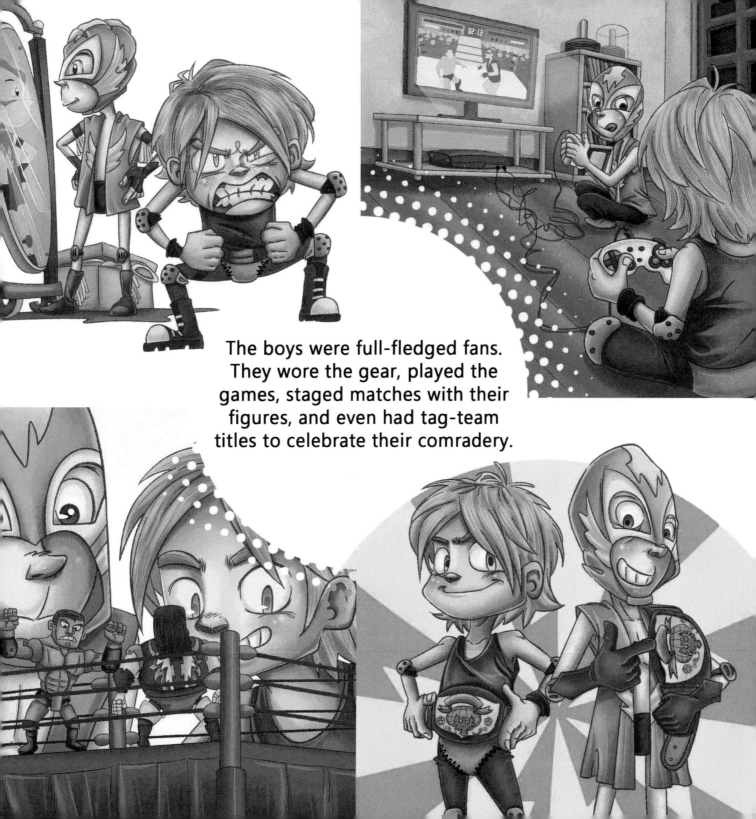

The boys were full-fledged fans. They wore the gear, played the games, staged matches with their figures, and even had tag-team titles to celebrate their comradery.

For Johnny's birthday one year, his dad took the two of them to a live Wild, Wild Warriors wrestling show. They got autographs, took pictures with all of the wrestlers, and even got to go into the ring. It was a dream come true, and clearly the coolest birthday ever!

When the new Wild, Wild Warriors video game came out, the first thing they did was create avatars of themselves as wrestlers.

Since Frankie was always honest and quite quiet (except for when he was around his best buddy), he created a noble ninja named *Ginzu*.

Johnny on the other hand was a bit of a boaster, flamboyant and full of life, so he decided his character would be named *The Bragger*.

This game is WILD!!! 10/10

THE BRAGGER
READY !!!

GINZU
READY !!!

OK   CANCEL

OK   CANCEL

1P   ANALOG   ANALOG   2P

The boys determined that Frankie would be the good guy or "baby face" and Johnny would be the bad guy or "heel."

They had such a blast creating their characters Johnny suggested bringing them to life.

Johnny searched the closet for some tough-looking threads. He settled on his Dad's old leather jacket and some stylish sunglasses. Frankie slipped on a bathrobe and hid his face behind the secrecy of a ski mask.

The boys felt powerful in their new attire, but having the right look was only part of the professional wrestling puzzle.

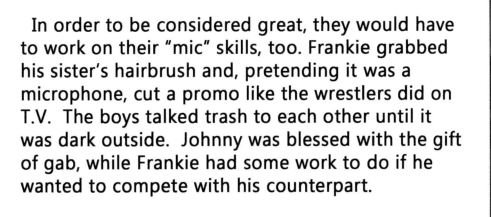

In order to be considered great, they would have to work on their "mic" skills, too. Frankie grabbed his sister's hairbrush and, pretending it was a microphone, cut a promo like the wrestlers did on T.V. The boys talked trash to each other until it was dark outside. Johnny was blessed with the gift of gab, while Frankie had some work to do if he wanted to compete with his counterpart.

They had hours of fun as wannabe-wrestlers, and before long, it was time for Johnny to go home.

The next day at school, Johnny had a great idea. He wanted to showcase all of their hard work and invite some friends over to watch a match between the two of them. When the bell rang, he rushed down the hall and told Frankie all about it.

"Frankie, it will be epic! Everyone will be so pumped after they see our sweet moves. Maybe they'll even want to join us in starting a wrestling federation of our own, just like we always dreamed. It will be AWESOME! What do you think?" Johnny asked with that familiar up-to-no-good look in his eyes.

"I don't know, Johnny. I enjoy having created costumes and speaking in front of an audience may even help me get over my shyness, but I'm not very athletic," Frankie admitted.

"We will just do some moves like they do on T.V. and everyone will go wild. Come on, PLEASE!" Johnny begged his buddy.

"It seems dangerous. I don't want either of us to get hurt. Plus, our moms will ground us forever if they find out. They always say that we aren't allowed to wrestle because we could get seriously injured," Frankie cautioned.

"Don't be such a baby. Besides, your mom will be at work anyway. She'll never even find out." Johnny knew just how stubborn his friend could be. If he wanted to convince him, he would have to play dirty, but that's what a "heel" did, anyway.

"Wrestlers are tough. Don't you want to be tough?" Johnny knew questioning Frankie's toughness would push his buttons and was his best bet to get what he wanted. Frankie was conflicted.

During lunch, Frankie slipped his *Ginzu* mask on, took a deep breath and climbed atop the table. His piercing eyes locked onto Johnny and he began to speak.

"*Bragger*, you boast about being the **BADDEST** around. You claim you can have anything you want, but you don't have the one thing that makes a true champion...**HEART!** I have lived my life by the code of the warrior. This Saturday, I am going to **SILENCE** your big mouth once and for all!"

Johnny never expected that his best friend could pull this off. All the kids in the cafeteria started "**OOHING**" and "**AHHING**." Johnny smiled and without missing a beat, picked up his spoon like it was a microphone.

"*Ginzu*, you've got to be kidding. You could practice kung fu for the rest of your life, but the only thing you will ever master is **LOSING**. I accept your challenge and come Saturday, I'm going to shatter your puny heart into a thousand pitiful pieces."

The cafeteria erupted with applause! The boys quickly made their exits, as to not arouse any suspicion about their main event match. To keep the illusion going that they were mortal enemies, they even avoided each other for the rest of the week. They had set the stage for a colossal confrontation.

The boys couldn't believe how quickly Saturday arrived. As they stood behind the curtain, adrenaline pumped through their veins.

"Frankie, this match has to be special. Listen to that crowd. They are going nuts!" Frankie's backyard was packed with at least 20 of their friends hooting and hollering.

"I've got an idea. Why don't you let me try out my new finishing move, *The Bragger Bomb*, during the match?" Johnny proposed.

This unexpected request sent a chill down Frankie's spine. He didn't like being put on the spot.

"I bet it won't hurt one bit. Besides, the mattress will be there to cushion your fall. Don't you trust me?" Johnny persisted.

To perform this move, Johnny would lift Frankie up over his head and slam him down on his back. Frankie had seen *Mr. Madness* do a similar move and it looked painful. He was frightened, but the cheers from the crowd numbed his fears. He knew that all the top wrestlers put on a good show for their fans and he didn't want to let anyone down, especially his best buddy.

Frankie gave Johnny a nod of approval before walking through the curtain. The chants of *"Ginzu"* echoed over his entrance music. The warm welcome from his fans calmed his nerves. He was ready to wrestle.

Next out was the bad boy himself, *The Bragger,* and he was showered with thunderous "BOOs." The referee, Frankie's little sister Claire, rang the bell and Ginzu bowed to his opponent.

That's when *The Bragger* hit him with a sneak attack and the match was underway.

The boys battled back and forth. Finally it was time for the big finish. With all his might, *The Bragger* picked *Ginzu* up above his head and dumped him down. He laid across him for the cover and when the referee counted to three, he leapt up to celebrate. In a twist, evil had triumphed over good. He expected to be "BOOed" out of the backyard, but instead, an eerie silence came over the crowd.

Johnny peered over his shoulder and noticed Frankie was still on the ground not moving a muscle. He knelt next to his fallen friend and, unsure how to handle the situation, he began to panic.

Luckily, Frankie's mother had just returned home from work. Mrs. Jackson dropped the groceries and rushed to Frankie's side. Her face was as pale as a ghost and tears rolled down her cheeks.

"Somebody call an ambulance!" she shrieked. Claire dialed 9-1-1.

"I didn't mean to hurt him. I'm sorry. I'm sorry. I'M SO SORRY!"

The boys' friends somberly shuffled out of the backyard to make room for the paramedics. Frankie's mother held his hand as they stabilized his neck and loaded him onto the stretcher.

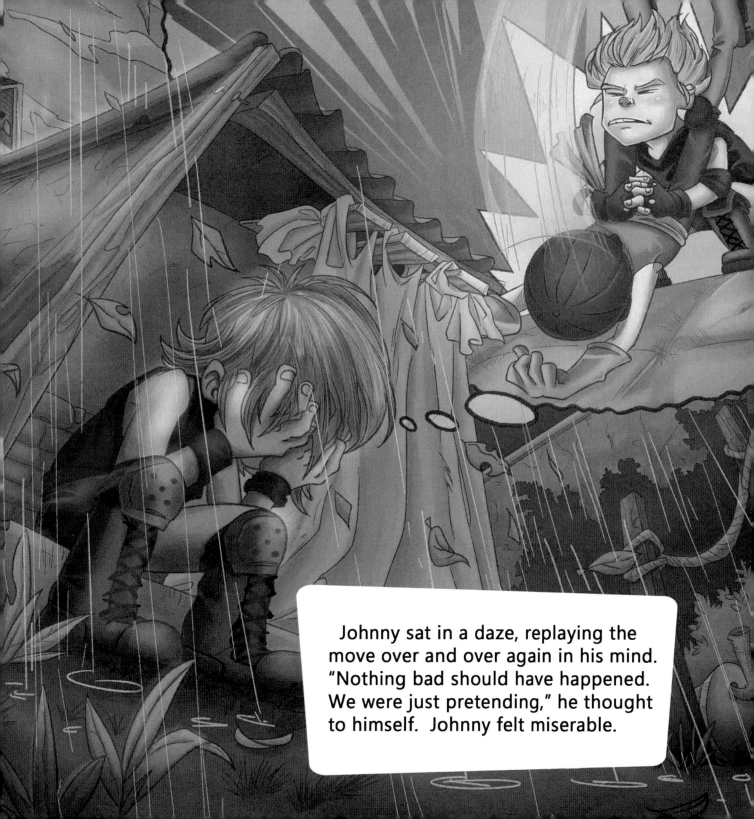

Johnny sat in a daze, replaying the move over and over again in his mind. "Nothing bad should have happened. We were just pretending," he thought to himself. Johnny felt miserable.

After a restless night, Johnny's father took him to see Frankie in the hospital. Johnny was met by the doctor upon his arrival.

"Frankie, I'm really sorry I pressured you into doing something you didn't want to do. That's not what best friends do. I'm really ashamed of myself and I hope you can forgive me. You're the toughest guy I know," Johnny confessed trying to hold back tears.

"You're my best bud and I should have listened to my gut. I never want to see that look on my mother's face again. It was terrible. From now on, let's just leave the wrestling to the pros," Frankie said with a smile.

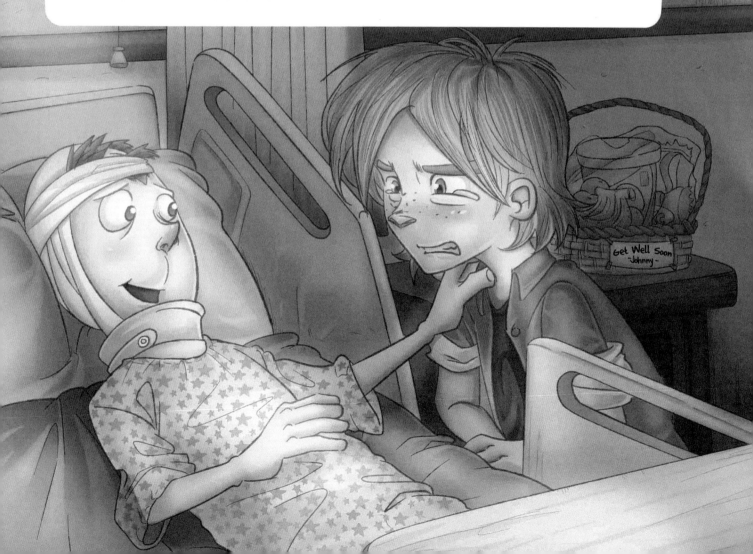

Johnny made sure to keep an eye on his buddy for the next few weeks. To make amends, he offered to help Frankie with whatever he needed, which is what good friends do. He also planned a special surprise for his pal.

"Frankie, I wanted to do something to show you just how much your friendship means to me," Johnny said as he flipped his laptop towards his friend.

Frankie's eyes widened with excitement. "Is that *Mr. Madness*?" Frankie blurted out.

"Just watch!" Johnny replied.

"Frankie, you are one tough dude. Johnny told me what the two of you did and although you guys are passionate about wrestling, it breaks my heart when I hear about someone getting hurt. I'll make you two a deal; if you guys leave the wrestling to *Mr. Madness* and the other Wild, Wild Warriors, you can have these two front row seats to watch me take on Ray the Destroyer this Saturday night. I hope I see you two Madmen there!" *Mr. Madness* proposed.

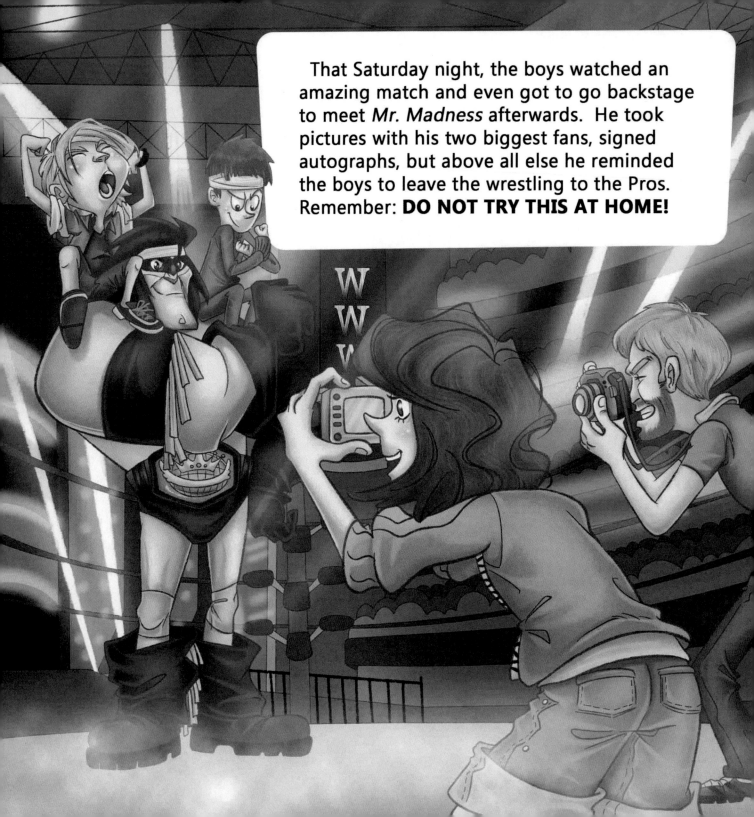